Stolen Away

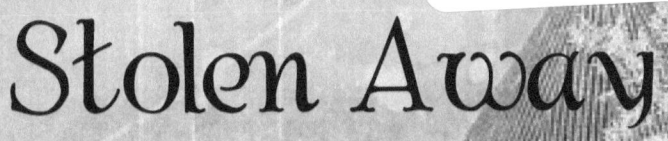

Prince and Pauper Press

Contact: Prince and Pauper Press, PO Box 386, South Sutton,
NH 03273 USA

Please visit our website www.princeandpauperpress.com

First Edition: April 2013

Carson, Jennifer 1975
Stolen Away : a collection of four short stories
Summary: Four young women stolen from their regular lives into
the magical unknown.

Cover design by Jennifer Carson
Interior layout by Jennifer Carson

ISBN 978-1-62251-998-9

Printed in the United States of America

Stolen Away

by

Jennifer Carson

For Chris

Table of Contents

The Knight

For Jess and Melissa

"This is ridiculous!" Sarah yelled as Mrs.Haney pulled the corset strings tight."Nothing exciting ever happens to good girls with good parents."

"You can't hang around waiting for Prince Charming," Mrs. Haney said. "You ain't a princess in a castle miss, but a servin' wench in a Renaissance fair tavern. You gotta make your own luck." She patted Sarah's shoulder consolingly.

"Gee, thanks for the sympathy," Sarah retorted.
Mrs. Haney shrugged her shoulders. "This ain't a fairy tale, and I ain't no fairy godmother."

Jennifer Carson

Sarah adjusted her skirts and laced her shoes. If she had been a real serving wench in the 1600's, at least she'd have the chance for a fairy tale ending. Some prince would come into the tavern and find himself mesmerized by her eyes. But all she ever got were drunken flirts or families with wide-eyed children dressed in plastic breast plates and carrying wooden swords. She turned to Mrs. Haney. "Well? Everything in the right place?"

Mrs. Haney's eyes traveled up her green skirts and over her red corset. Sarah had left her hair down today—her waist-long butterscotch-colored hair was her best feature. Mrs. Haney smiled. "A right proper serving wench you be! Now, get out there and serve those ales."

Sarah stuck her tongue out playfully at Mrs. Haney and stepped through the dressing room door and into the raucous tavern. It was only noon, but because of the drizzle and the sodden earth the few faire patrons that had braved the day were already wild in their cups. Some of them got so wrapped up in the pretend-ness of it all that they actually believed they were in the sixteenth century. She was constantly fighting off grabbing hands and suggestive words. But the tips were worth it.

It was dim and warm in the tavern, with a small fire built up in the hearth to ward off the autumn chill. She was filling the cups of a bunch of rowdy college boys when she noticed the knight enter.

He filled the doorway with his broad, armored shoulders and paused, assessing the crowd. Then he pushed back his damp hood. The firelight framing him shone off his chestnut brown hair, which flowed in waves over his shoulders. His surcoat was a brilliant blue with a large crescent moon over his heart. The sleeves of his hauberk shone like polished silver. Sarah was struck dumb. He looked authentic. She wondered where he got his suit of mail—surely work that good didn't come from Donny and Phil and their "Mailboys" booth.

Sarah felt a push from behind. "Go on," Mrs. Haney whispered. "There's something exciting."

Stumbling forward, Sarah made her way through the crowd toward the knight. She giggled. It struck her as funny calling him a knight. She wondered what he really was—a carpenter, an engineer, a grocery bagger? He could be anything in real life. Sometimes it was shocking to hear what a faire patron really did during the week. "You seem a bit lost, sir knight. May I help you find a seat? A cup of ale perhaps?"

The knight bowed his head. "You are most gracious, Milady." He reached for her hand and placed his soft lips above her knuckles. Sarah caught her breath and the knight looked up. His green eyes searched her face.

"I'm not a lady," Sarah stuttered. "Just a serving wench." She laughed nervously and pulled her hand out of his grasp.

"You are too beautiful to be just a serving wench," the knight said. He smiled a crooked little grin. "What else are you?"

"Flabbergasted." Sarah sighed.

"That is your surname? Flabbergasted?" The knight's eyebrows knit together.

Sarah laughed again. "Oh, no. My name is Sarah. Farmington is my surname."

"A royal line for sure." The knight looked over her shoulder, scanning the room.

Sarah turned and surveyed the room too. "Are you looking for someone? Your comrades in arms or your girlfriend, perhaps?"

"Girlfriend?" The knight had a puzzled look on his face.

Sarah rolled her eyes. "Your lady, I meant. Are you looking for your lady?"

"I seem to be in the wrong place." The knight shook his head. "I don't really remember how I came to be here."

Sarah put her arm through his and led him to an empty booth. "Maybe you were hit a little hard when you were jousting. You sit right here. I'll walkie the medics."

"What is walkie?"

Sarah rolled her eyes again. People working the faire were always so uppity about keeping it real. "I beg your pardon, knight. I shall keep my tongue in check and speak the language of the King."

He nodded. "May I take you up on that ale? Perhaps it will help clear my head."

Sarah raised her eyebrows. Ale to help clear the head? That was a new one. "Sit tight." She pushed her way to the dressing room and grabbed the walkie-talkie from the charging station. It crackled as she pushed the button. "This is Sarah from the Man O'War Tavern. We need a medic. I think we have a knight who's knocked himself silly. He can't remember how he got over here."

"You sure you didn't get him drunk?" Gary, the medic on duty, cackled into the radio.

Sarah pushed the button in with a sigh. "I haven't even served him yet."

Hooting laughter came through the small speaker. "Sure! I know how you tavern wenches are!"

"Are you coming or not, Gary?"

"I'll be there in two shakes of a wenches tail," the medic answered.

Sarah slammed the radio into its charger. It didn't matter if they were stall muckers or doctors—men were all the same. She took a deep breath and walked back into the tavern. Pulling a ceramic mug from a hook she filled it with ale from the tap.

Mrs. Haney gave her ribs a little rubbing with her elbow as she joined her at the draft machine. "So, what's his story?"

Sarah shrugged her shoulders. "I'm not sure yet. I think he wandered in from the joust. He might have a concussion. He can't remember how he got here."

Mrs. Haney cocked her head. "But there ain't no jousting today. Too wet for the horses." She took her brimming full mug and was off again.

Sarah glanced at the knight. He had the greatest costumer ever. She couldn't remember seeing another so well made and from period appropriate fabrics and colors too. She carried the ale over to the knight and set it in front of him. "You never told me your name."

The knight pushed his hair from his face. "Brannock."

"Is that your first name or your surname?"

"Michael is what my mother called me."

"Great." Sarah flung her tresses over her shoulder. "Well, Michael, the medic is coming to take a look at you. He'll see if you have a concussion from the joust."

"But I wasn't jousting." He shook his head, a dreamy look clouding his face.

"What were you doing then, before you came into the tavern?" Sarah slid into the other side of the booth, facing the knight. She would just sit here until Gary showed up.

"I was riding on a path at the edge of the forest near the castle, patrolling the cities borders. I had just passed through the crumbling section of a stone wall when I heard a cry. So I dismounted and followed the sound into the forest."

"And then?" Sarah prompted. She'd been watching his face as he spoke, wracking her brain for the signs of a concussion—weren't his pupils supposed to be really small? Really big? She couldn't remember. What was taking Gary so long?

"And then I came out into a clearing and found myself in this small village." Michael drained the ale and set the mug down on the table. He ran his thumb over the smooth pottery. "This is fantastic workmanship. Do you have your own potter?"

"No, they just come from some catalog." Sarah waved her hand in dismissal.

"Catalog?" The knight raised his brows in askance.

"Yeah, you know. Like the Museum Replica catalog or something."

The knight shook his head. "I'm trying to make sense of all these strange words you keep using… Am I in the land of the fae?"

Michael didn't wait for her to answer. "That can be the only explanation." His fist slammed down on the tabletop as he rose in the booth. "And now I'm stuck because I drank the ale. Tell me, are you a nymph? Will you change from your beautiful form and make me your slave now that you have me trapped?"

"That isn't a bad idea." Sarah giggled nervously at the attention he had drawn from the other patrons. She slowly stood and raised her hands, palms out toward him. "But alas, I am not fae, and I have no magical powers."

His gaze was intense, as if he either found her fascinating or was trying to see into her soul. He must have knocked himself completely looney. That was the only reason she could think of for his strange behavior. An inexplicable thought floated from the back of her mind. Before she could stop herself she blurted out, "What year is it?"

Michael breathed out a noble sigh and slumped in the booth. "It is the reign of Edward III, about 1348 in the year of our Lord."

Sarah stood abruptly, knocking her hipbone on a sharp corner of the table. "Ouch!" Her hands went to her hip and pressed the spot as he doubled over. She was going to have a nice bruise.

Michael swiftly stood and caught her arms. "Are you alright, Milady?"

She shooed him away. "I'll be fine. Man! That hurt."

The tavern door swung open and Gary strolled in, whistling.

"Finally!" Sarah yelled, a little more crossly than was needed.

Gary grinned as he pushed his way through the crowd, his black leather bag swaying in his hand. "Couldn't wait to see me, eh?"

Michael straightened his shoulders and squared up to the medic. "You should take a look at Milady Sarah first. I'm afraid she took a great hit from the table."

Gary raised his eyebrows and turned to Sarah. "Oh? A rough shift already?"

"Shut up, Gary. I just hit my hip on the table corner when I stood up." She gestured to the knight. "This is Michael. He says he wasn't jousting but he doesn't know how he got here." Sarah paused. She wasn't sure if she should tell him the rest. It might be important though. She decided to leave the fairies out of it. "And he thinks the year is 1348."

"Does it look like 1348 to you?" Gary asked Michael.

"There are some strange things in this village."

Gary put his hand on the knight's shoulder and guided him back into the booth. He set his bag on the table and unzipped it. After rummaging around a bit Gary pulled out an ophthalmoscope and shined the light in the knight's eyes.

Michael pulled back and flung his arms up over his face. "What kind of devilry is this?"

Gary laughed. "You can put away the rennie antics. It's just a light so I can see how your pupils react."

"My what?"

Michael looked as if he was about to jump over the table and flee for his life. Sarah sat on the tabletop and reached for his hand. He turned to her, searching for understanding.

She squeezed his hand reassuringly. The uneasy look on his face reminded her of when she had to take the little neighbor boy to the dentist for a filing because his mom couldn't get the time off of work. "The ophthalmoscope is a tool that doctors use to see how your eyes react to the light. Have you never been to an optometrist?"

Michael shook his head.

"Don't worry, it doesn't hurt." She sat up straight. "Gary, do it to me first, so he can see what will happen."

"You're joking, right?" Gary smirked. "He's not a five year old."

Sarah pinched her lips together and gave him a look. "Do it!"

Gary rolled his eyes and flashed the light in her face, his cinnamon breath gently touching her cheeks as he peered into her eyes. He must have popped in a few breath mints on his way over. She sighed internally. There was no way that was going to happen. *Ever*.

"See?" Sarah said to Michael when Gary pulled away. "Not a big deal. Will you let Gary look at your eyes now?"

The knight shifted uncomfortably in the booth. "You won't be putting any spells on me, sorcerer?"

Gary and Sarah exchanged a grin. "No spells, you have my word," Gary said. "As you can see, Sarah is totally in control of herself."

Michael pulled himself forward in the booth and tilted his head back a little. Gary bent and peered into his eyes one at a time. "Hmm…interesting."

"What?" asked Sarah.

"No sign of a concussion."

Sarah's heart leapt into her throat. "Were you expecting one?"

Gary straightened and dropped his light back in his medic bag. "You weren't?"

Sarah shrugged her shoulders. A concussion was the only rational explanation she could think of. She didn't really believe in magic or time travel or any of that fantasy stuff, although it was fun to pretend. There was something about Michael though that didn't strike her as pretending.

"I'll need you to take off that mail. Do you need help removing it?" Gary asked the knight.

"No." Michael stood and pulled off his surcoat.

Sarah instinctively reached for it. The material was heavy. She scrutinized the stitching of the moon. It was clear that the finely spaced stitches worked in gold thread, were done by hand. Who ever made this surcoat knew what they were doing and spent numerous hours on the task. The knight's hauberk dropped with a rasping clang to the wooden floor. Michael wore a dark blue jupon underneath. It looked as if it had seen better days. The tight fitting sleeveless shirt was frayed at the shoulders and stained heavily. He glanced at Sarah with a look of apology. "My newer jupon was with the laundress."

"And your mantle? Was that with the laundress as well?" Gary teased him.

"I threw it over my horse when I dismounted. I didn't want it to get tangled in the forest briars."

"Didn't you read the signs that said to stay on the path?" Gary asked.

"There was no path in the forest I was in," Michael said, an indignant tone entering his voice. "Anyway, a knight of the Garter wanders where he pleases."

"Oooh, a knight of the Garter?" Gary smirked. "Well, we are aiming high aren't we? Lift your arms."

Michael lifted his arms and rolled his head back in exasperation. "There is nothing wrong with me. I feel perfectly healthy."

Sarah thought he looked perfectly healthy too. Her gaze traveled from his well-built shoulders, down his muscled trunk and over his legs. Encircling his left knee was a blue belt made of silk. She ran her fingers over it's gilt buckles and bent to admire the finely worked gold embroidery. Even the tiniest details of his costume were true to history. The hair on the back of her nape rose as a chill spiraled down her backbone. What if he wasn't pretending?

"Well, I agree," Gary said.

Sarah straightened and suddenly felt a bit woozy. Was Gary reading her mind?

"You are the picture of perfect health," the medic continued. "And a superb actor."

Sarah slumped into the booth, her hands clenching Michael's surcoat. This couldn't be real. Mrs. Haney's words rang in her ears. *This isn't a fairy tale.*

Gary zipped his bag and slung it over his shoulder. He turned and the crowd parted for him. "Nice to meet you, Michael, of the Order of the Garter." His deep-throated laughter filled the tavern. "Carry on!"

Michael pulled his coat of mail over his head and settled it onto his shoulders. "Is something the matter, Milady?" He crouched in front of her and when Sarah lifted her head his brow was creased with worry.

"You really aren't from here, are you?"

"I was born in St. Albans, just north of London. But now I live near the castle at Windsor on a small estate granted to me by Prince Edward."

Could he truly be a companion of the Black Prince Edward? But time travel and wormholes and fairy tales weren't actually real. Were they?

"Would you be able to retrace your steps through the forest? I'd like to see where you turned off." Sarah held out Michael's surcoat. He smiled and let her guide it over his head and mailed arms.

"I'd be delighted to take a turn with you." He stood and held out his hand. Sarah placed her hand in his. She could feel the rough callouses on his palms and the strength in his fingers as he led her across the tavern.

"Hey! Sarah!" Mrs. Haney yelled across the room. "Y'er shift ain't over till 7!"

Sarah waved and smiled over her shoulder. "Just taking a quick walk, Mrs. Haney!"

The wind raced through the shop facades and trees scattered about the faire grounds. A wedding party was just coming out of the chapel and the courtyard stage area was full of guests enjoying the juggling troupe. The faire really was a magical place.

"Is it always so busy in this hamlet?" Michael asked.

Sarah grinned. "Yes, unless it is pouring rain. Then everything turns to mud and the patrons stay at home and we don't make any money."

"I don't think I'd like to live in such a busy place, but I can see the charm for a tavern mistress. Crowds do mean profits."

"Yes, they do, but I often dream of a quiet home on a rolling pasture. I'm not like most girls who dream of marrying a prince. I'd rather have the fire-hardened blacksmith or the wind-blown sailor."

"Not a knight?" Michael asked.

Sarah lowered her eyes. A blush raced up her neck and settled in her cheeks. "A knight would do too."

Michael smiled and drew her onto the path that led to the patron parking lots. "This is where I came through to your village." The knight pointed up the path a bit to a tree that was decorated with many bits and baubles of shinning glass. "There! At the witch's tree. That's where I came out of the forest." Michael led her to the witch's tree and pointed to the trampled brush. "See, you can still see my path."

She grasped the knight's arm tighter. Would she allow herself to believe in fairy tales? In time travel? Her heart pounded against her corset. "Can you take me to the castle?"

"Of course." He led her through the forest, following his brushy trail. Sarah soon heard a whicker and when the forest opened up into a small meadow sunlight shimmered off the mane of a white horse. The drizzling rain was gone. A chill autumn breeze tickled the edges of a blue mantle draped across the horse's back.

"This can't be real," Sarah murmured as goosebumps rose on her arms. She stroked the velvet nose of the horse. It was warm and damp.

It felt real.

"Shall we, Milady?" Michael was holding the mantle open, expecting to wrap her in its folds. His face had a genuine expression of kindness.

Sarah let him clasp the heavy mantle around her shoulders. She bit her lip in disbelief as he easily lifted her up into the saddle. After he climbed up behind her, she nestled into the knight's warm chest. He clicked his tongue and the horse strode to the edge of the meadow and through a gap in a crumbled stone wall.

"Michael, do you believe in fairy tales?" she asked.

The knight encircled her in his arms as he grabbed the rein. His breath tickled against her ear. "Believe in fairy tales? Doesn't everyone?"

Sarah smiled as the tall spire of a castle came into view. She'd been wrong about everything.

Fairy tales.

Wormholes.

And exciting things happening to good girls with good parents.

A Light of Victory

for my own scottish rake

Bess set a drink before Mr. Bauer, against her better judgment. Her father would probably have to tie him to his saddle in order to get him home again tonight. No matter—whether Mr. Bauer made it home or not, it was coin in her father's pocket.

"Oh, Bess. You're a mighty piece of work, ain't ye?" Her skirts stirred and a rough hand grabbed her buttock as Gibbons slid into the booth. "Why don't ye warm me bed tonight?"

She swayed her hips away from the offender, wishing she could dig her elbow into his side or crush his toes under her heel. "I'd appreciate if you would remember, Mr. Gibbons, that my father runs a tavern, not a whorehouse."

Sitting across the table from Gibbons was Mr. Ledbetter. When he smiled, strings of white mucus pulled at the corners of his mouth. "Well, if you won't warm ole' Gibbons's bed, miss, maybe you'll warm mine!" A chorus of guffaws and table pounding from the men in the tavern echoed off the wood-paneled walls.

"The only thing that ought to warm your bed, Mr. Ledbetter, is a warming pan." Bess turned from the table and made her way through the crowd toward the bar, where her father was polishing the cutlery.

The dripping juices from the roasting boar sizzled in the flames of the cooking hearth. Her stomach rumbled at the savory smell of the meat, but she'd have to wait until the last customer had eaten his fill; then she and her father could eat if some were left.

Bess turned the spit and wiped the grease from her hands onto her apron. "What is it about ale that makes men behave like feral dogs?" She tossed some dirty mugs into the washbasin and scrubbed them with a vengeance.

Her father shook his head. "I'm sorry, lass, I know it's not the right place for ye to be working, but there's no choice. If I had the money, I'd hire a server, and you could work in a proper household."

Bess tossed the rag on the counter. "I don't think I've wiped my arse as many times as he's groped it."

Was it old Gibbons again?" Her father asked. "I'd like to grope the seat of his pants and toss him out the door, but you know we count on his coin and his good graces to stay in business."

Bess stared out the window. The gusty wind plucked the leaves from the trees like a child robbing the biscuit jar. Soon the trees would be nothing but dark, skeletal fingers reaching into the heavens. She sighed. "Yes, I understand. And it's not just Gibbons, but half a dozen other men as well. You can't tell me you don't see it."

Her father rubbed his hand across his forehead. "Perhaps it is time for Nicholas and I to have a talk. Is he coming back into town tonight?"

Bess fiddled with the bauble on her necklace. She had spent days trying not to think about Nicholas while he was away, but every time the tavern door opened her heart flipped with excitement and then fell into disappointment when it wasn't him. "I'm not sure if he will be back tonight, though I hope so. He said he would be in Fife for a few days and would send post if he had to stay longer."

"Wench!"

Bess's eyes flicked to the back corner table where Gibbons smirked and held his mug aloft.

Her father's meaty fist pounded on the counter. He pointed to Mr. Gibbons. "It's Miss. Haverstock to you, Gibbons. And if ye put your paws on my daughter again, I won't wait to fetch the bobby but put you in the stocks meself!"

"Thanks, Da," Bess whispered as she grabbed another round of mugs brimming with ale. The men's stares were heavy as she sauntered to the booth. As she set the last cup before Gibbons she smiled. The light of a small victory hovered around her. "Will that be all for you tonight, gentlemen?" She stressed the last word.

"That's all for this occasion, Miss Haverstock," Gibbons answered with a sardonic curl to his lip. "Perhaps on another occasion you can provide us with more friendly service."

"I doubt you could rise to the occasion, Mr. Gibbons. I'm afraid a friendly smile and a cup of ale is all you'll be served in my father's establishment." Bess turned on her heel and crossed the room. No new patrons had entered the tavern for quite a while; the dinner rush had fizzled out and evening was moving into night. She grabbed the broom from the corner and swept the crumbs and dried mud out from under the empty tables. She tried to keep her mind on her work, but thoughts of Nicholas kept interrupting her chores.

"You really shouldn't talk to Mr.Gibbons that way."

Bess stiffened. The moist whisperings of Frasier, the ostler, brushed against her ear. She drew a breath from her mouth to avoid the soured milk smell of him and turned, placing the broom between her and the mousey man. "He shouldn't speak to me that way."

Frasier smoothed his limp hair from his forehead with a thin shaky hand and shuffled closer. "I would never speak to you that way." His eyes shifted over her shoulder and then to her breasts. "Gibbons is a powerful man in this town though. Could put your father out of business."

Bess stepped back. She didn't like Frasier, but she wasn't about to let him bait her with ridiculous notions. "Everyone knows my father's inn is the best in the village."

"Yes, and he uses his good reputation to his advantage, doesn't he?" Frasier closed the space between them. The sour milk smell engulfed her like flames overwhelm a letter tossed into the hearth. "I heard a rumor he houses unsavories. Highwaymen and the like."

"And where would this rumor come from?" Bess asked. "An ostler perhaps?"

Frasier snorted. "No one cares who starts a rumor. And no one cares to find the truth behind the whispers. Perhaps your father should stop welcoming thieves to his door."

Bess whispered fiercely through her teeth, "My father doesn't welcome thieves or highwaymen or any other unsavories."

"Poor Bess," Frasier whispered back. "So young and naïve. They haven't even told you the truth about your dear, pretty Nicholas. Have they?"

Bess held her ground but her heart strained against its cage.

The ostler raised a finger to stroke the bauble hanging from Bess's neck. "Ever wonder where he gets those pretty trinkets he gives you?"

Bess had heard enough. What did the ostler know about Nicholas that she didn't? She brushed his hand away. "You would do well to remember your position. I'm sure these gentlemen will need their horses saddled and ready before the hour is up. You should see to it, since that is what my father pays you to do."

The ostler's eyes darted over her shoulder, then his gaze dropped to the floorboards. "Yes, perhaps I ought to." He shuffled away, shoulders bent like an overused crop. Bess stared after him. What would an ostler know about her father's company? She glanced at the table in the corner. Mr. Gibbons raised his cup to her before taking a swallow of ale.

His fixed stare made the hair at the nape of her neck stand on end.

Bess swept the pile of dirt and crumbs into the hearth as Mr. Gibbons took his leave from Mr. Bauer, whose head was nodding in his cup. Mr. Ledbetter, not quite as drunk as Mr. Bauer, leered at her from across the room, a feeble wave the only acknowlegment of Mr. Gibbons's departure. A feeling of unease grew in Bess's chest. The ostler, Gibbons, and his cronies were going to cause trouble. She could feel it.

Bess returned the broom against the wall, not interested in trying to keep busy anymore. Nicholas would've come by now, if he was coming. The floors were clean and most of the dishes washed.

She stopped her father as he latched the tavern door behind Gibbons. "Will you be all right if I head to bed? I can finish washing the tables in the morning when I'm not so tired."

Her father led her across the room, his warm hand pressed against the small of her back. "Go off with ye, wash up, it's been a long day. I'll bring up a plate when I get these two gone for the night. The roast sure smelt good today, didn't it? Just like your mother used to cook."

Bess nodded and kissed her father's ruddy cheek. "I'm sure it's delicious." She climbed the narrow set of stairs to the second-story living space. Her mother had been gone for twelve years, leaving her father to bring up a daughter by himself.

She'd had a governess when she was little, but when she turned fourteen three years ago her father had let the governess go and used the wages to hire the ostler. She shivered at the thought of Frasier. He was always shuffling about in the shadows and muttering to himself. She had felt empathy for the young man when her father had first hired him and made every effort to make him feel at home. He'd been raised in a church orphanage and knew no mother or father. But he'd proved himself to be a skulking trouble monger ever since, and her sympathy for his poor upbringing had long since disappeared.

She stripped off her blouse before reaching her room. It was stained and smelled of stale ale and smoke. The air gripped her skin with its icy fingers and she rushed to push her bedroom door open. The hearth in her room was blazing and the heavy curtains that enveloped her four-poster bed were tied back to allow the warmth from the fire to spread throughout the room. She hated the fact that Frasier was in her private space every day, but she was grateful for the fire that warmed her chamber. She set a pot of fresh water near the hearth to warm it and when it began to steam, poured it into the wash basin, adding a little cold water from the pitcher on the bed stand.

The moon rose, full and glorious, filling her room with a fragile light. She could see the road from Fife twisting through the moors, its cobbled surface shining in the moonlight. She closed the shutters against peering eyes and washed the smell of smoke and ale from her skin.

Bess sat on the edge of her bed plaiting a red ribbon into her freshly washed hair. The ribbon had been a gift from her father on her birthday. The wind gusted against the window, rattling the pane, but another sound was on the wind as well. She held her breath and strained her ears. A whistle rose to her window, like the flower vines that twist up the trellis in the summer. She rushed to push the shutters aside and peered into the courtyard.

Below, a dark stallion pranced underneath his rider. Clouds of ethereal steam billowed around the pair, making horse and rider look as if they had ridden from the hills of faerieland itself. Nicholas removed his cocked hat, turned his face to the window and whistled his tune again. Bess threw open the sash. "Nicholas! You're back."

"I'm sorry, Bess. I didn't think it would be this late when I arrived."

Bess shook her head. "It doesn't matter. I'm just glad you're back. Was the journey successful?"

"Yes." He tied his reign to the trellis and tested the strength of the crisscrossed slats.

Bess leaned out of the window. "What are you doing? What if someone sees you?"

As Nicholas scurried up the trellis, the moonlight danced in his eyes. His warm breath tickled her lips. "After tomorrow, it won't matter if someone sees me." He tumbled through the window and onto the floor. Bess rushed into his embrace.

"I've missed you, sweetness," he breathed in her ear.

A knock sounded at the bedroom door and Bess pulled away in panic, searching the room for a way to disguise her lover.

"I've got yer plate, Bess, open up!" her father called.

"Coming, Da!" She shooed Nicholas under the bed, stood up, brushed the dust from her nightgown, and checked to see if Nicholas's feet were hidden before pulling the door open. Her father pranced in, humming a tune, with a flower clenched between his teeth. He set the plate of food on her dressing table and flourished his hand as if he was a grand Spanish dancer. Bess couldn't help but giggle at his antics. "Oh, Da. Such the fool you play." She plucked the wilting flower from his hand. "Perhaps you should think of a change in career."

Her father shook his head and pecked his daughter on the cheek. "Nah, I'm too old to learn how to do cartwheels for the queen." He shivered. "Good lord girl, it's cold in here!

Why is your window open?" He moved to the window and latched it closed, then stirred the coals in the hearth, bending with a groan to place another log into the fire.

Bess rubbed her father's back. "I'll do that, Da. You go on to bed."

"Dear Bess. You are too good to your old Da." He walked into the hall and turned to shut the door behind him. "Good night. Sweet dreams."

"Good night." Bess breathed a sigh of relief as the door latched.

Nicholas sneezed.

"Bless you!" her father called from the hallway.

Bess giggled as Nicholas slid out from under the bed. "Well, that was close."

"Too close. My heart almost leapt out of my throat when Da knocked." She set the plate on the edge of the bed and patted the mattress. "Come, share my dinner. There's too much here for just me."

Nicholas sat next to her and pulled the ribbon from her hair, loosening the radiant blue-black braid. Her hair cascaded over her shoulder and he wound his fingers in it, pulling the

41

silky lengths to his cheek. He breathed in her scent. "Just the smell of you soothes my hunger."

Bess felt a flush crawl up her neck and spread to her cheeks. She pushed against his shoulder. "Oh, be serious. You must be famished after the long ride from Fife."

"I am, but not for food." His intense gaze burned into her soul. His hand moved to his breast coat pocket. He pulled out a ring, an oval ruby cradled in gold. Nicholas picked up her hand and slid the ring on her finger. "A perfect fit."

Bess drew in a breath. It was the most beautiful thing she'd ever seen. The ostler's words prickled in the back of her mind. "Where did you get it?"

Nicholas dismissed her question with a wave of his hand. "Some English chap needed a loan. I bought it off of him."

Bess extended her hand and admired the way the firelight danced on the surface of the jewel. "I can't accept it. It is too much."

Nicholas curled her fingers down and clasped her hand in his. "You will keep it. It belongs to you, just like my heart." He kissed her until she forgot about her protests, then he wound the hair ribbon loosely around his fingers and nested it in the empty spot in his pocket where the ring used to sit. "Tomorrow I will ask your father for your hand in marriage, and this time he will say yes."

Below, the horse whinnied and shifted his weight, hooves stamping on the cobblestones. Nicholas turned to the window, listening. "I have to go now, but I'll be back tomorrow."

"Do you have to leave?" Bess pouted. "You just got here."

His warm hand stroked her hair. "I must. Something makes my mount uneasy. If it's one thing I've learned on the road, it's to pay attention to the animals." He rose from the bed and pushed the shutters veiling the window aside. Moonlight painted silver rays along the floor.

Bess joined him at the window and peered out. The uneasy feeling she'd had earlier returned to settle in her chest. "What danger could there be?"

Nicholas pointed to a shadow shuffling at the edge of the moorland. "I suspect it has something to do with him."

"The ostler!" Bess clenched her fists. She would recognize that awkward gait anywhere. Her disgust for

Frasier boiled over. "Father must get rid of him before he causes trouble. I hate that watery-eyed, ill-mannered boor."

"Hate is a rather ugly word for such a pretty mouth."

"But hate him I do," Bess said.

Nicholas raised her chin with a finger and kissed her again. "If I'm not back before noon," he whispered, "then I had to take precautions. The roads are perilous with King George's men lurking everywhere and suspecting every Scottish lad. If I am delayed, or hounded through the day, then watch for me by the moonlight."

"If you do not come at morning or at noon, I'll leave a candle burning in the window," Bess said as he lifted the sash and climbed onto the trellis. With sure footing, he shimmied down to his horse and planted his feet firmly in the stirrups. Nicholas blew one last kiss to Bess before galloping away.

Nicholas did not return in the morning, and Bess did her best to attend to her chores. By noon her nerves made her hands shake so, she was almost unable to pour a mug of ale without spilling. Her father had been eyeing her all day.

"Are you ill, Bess?" her father finally asked.

"No, Da." Bess shook her head. "I'm just all a-jangle today."

Father patted her shoulder. "I can see that. You've scrubbed the same spot on the counter for the last five minutes. Soon there will be no finish left."

Bess dropped the rag and wiped her hands on her apron. "I'm sorry, Da. My head keeps flying off into the clouds. I'm worried, Da—" Bess startled as the front doors burst open. Soldiers marched in, lining up against the walls. The ostler, who'd been lingering near the fire, took to the shadows and disappeared.

Her father exchanged an uneasy glance with Bess. "What's the meaning of this?" he said to the officer.

The captain approached the bar. "Food and drink for the men are needed. Tell the other customers to leave."

Her father clenched his fists and stared at the captain. When the soldier made no concession, her father cleared his throat and spoke to her from between stiff jaws. "You heard him, Bess, tell the others we are closing. They can settle up tomorrow."

Bess skirted around the counter, wary of the soldiers standing guard. She cleared the plates and cups of the customers she dismissed. They urgently whispered to her, asking questions Bess had no answers to.

"At ease, gentlemen," the captain commanded. "Except for you, Barker, and your two cronies there. You take the girl to the room facing the road and gag her. We don't want her warning him."

Two soldiers grabbed Bess, each grasping an arm. The dishes she'd been carrying scattered and broke on the floor. Her father came over the bar like a puma leaping over Hadrian's wall. The captain grabbed him and twisted his arm behind his back. He struggled and the soldier brandished a knife. The sharp edge glinted under her father's chin.

"You can't do this!" Bess' sobs lodged in her throat. Tears sprang to her eyes as the two soldiers dragged her from the tavern and up the stairs. She could hear her father pleading with the army captain, his voice rough and strained.

Barker, the soldier put in charge, kicked open the door of Bess's chamber. Frasier was restocking the wood by the hearth. Barker pointed to him. "You, ostler, take the sheet off the bed and gag her, then tie her to the bed post."

Bess thrashed against her captors while Frasier pulled the sheet from her mattress and tore it into strips, all the while a smirk playing on his face.

"Is this what you wanted, Frasier?" Bess whispered. "Did Gibbons talk you into this?"

The ostler couldn't meet her eyes. "I did it for you, Bess, because I love you. That thief, Nicholas, doesn't deserve the horse he rides, let alone the prettiest filly in town." He dipped toward her, his moist lips hesitating near hers.

Bess took the opportunity to turn her face. "If you truly loved me, you wouldn't be doing this."

Frasier's mouth pulled into a thin line. He wrapped the end of the linen strip around his hand. "I shoveled manure, split wood and kept your chamber warm these past four years. I've borne you treating me as lower than the horses I cared for in the hopes that you would see the truth."

Bess looked into his watery eyes. "My sympathy for your poor upbringing ended when you began to feel entitled to more than your fair share," Bess said. "My father paid you more than what you deserved and still you demanded more. I was never part of the bargain."

Frasier bowed his head. "You still spurn me for a pretty thief."

"Just do it, already. It's obvious she has no feelings for you, ostler," Barker said. He pushed the shutters away from the window.   The sun was setting over the moors, bathing the pale October fields in a red blaze.

Bess cried out as Frasier forced his lips upon hers. Then he jammed the material over her face, cutting into the sides of her mouth. He pulled the knot tight against her scalp. The soldiers held her tight against the bedpost while the ostler tied another strip around her chest, fastening her arms tight to her sides. Another strip held her legs tight to the bottom of the bedpost. The floor was cold beneath her bare feet.

Barker turned from the window. "That will be all, Frasier."

Bess struggled against the bindings. Her breath came fast and shallow. Her teeth clenched the gag. She couldn't scream as the ostler trailed his dirty fingers over her breast. He gathered the thin fabric of her blouse in his hands and buried his face in its folds. A sudden jerk ripped her blouse down the center. His mouth bit into her delicate skin. Bess struggled at the bindings holding her captive and tried to kick Frasier, but her legs were tied tight.

Barker slapped a heavy hand on the ostler's shoulder. "I said that's enough. There will be time for that later. After our task is finished she'll be in need of a new lover."

Frasier stepped away with reluctance, wiping the corner of his mouth with a dirty hand. He shuffled from the room and Bess heard the door latch behind him.

Barker stepped closer to her, thick fingers tracing the line of her jaw. "Now, we can't have a sweet thing like you doing anything to make me ruin that pretty face, can we?"

Bess narrowed her eyes. If she could have spit on him she would have. The soldier placed the barrel of his musket under her exposed breast, the cold steel branding her skin. Goosebumps rose over her body like the pox. Barker tied the musket to her side. The click of the hammer echoed in her ears. The slight smell of sulfer wafted from the barrel.

"Now, keep good watch," Barker whispered, tucking a wayward curl behind her ear. His lips grazed her neck.

Bess wept as she struggled against the bindings. Barker laughed at her futile attempts to gain freedom. The other two soldiers knelt at the window casement and inspected their firearms. Barker backed away and paced the room, back and forth, his hands clasped behind his back.

With the soldiers busy watching the road, Bess strained against the binding constricting her arms. The moon rose and hung like a silver orb in the night sky, lighting the road Nicholas would ride.

Barker stopped his pacing and chewed his bottom lip.

Bess returned his stare. Beads of sweat trickled down the side of her face. She tried not to look at the candle standing forlorn and unlit in the windowsill, but her eyes betrayed her.

The soldier looked from Bess to the window and back. He unclasped his hands and smoothed his mustache with his fingers.

Nicholas didn't know the redcoats were waiting for him at the inn, muskets trained on the rise. They would catch him unaware and shoot him down. Bess looked at the candle again. She prayed Nicholas would see that it did not burn as she had promised. That he would think twice before coming to the inn. She closed her eyes, and taking a deep breath, sent her prayer to the heavens.

"Light that candle in the window," Barker commanded. "I have a feeling he will be expecting it."

New tears pricked Bess's eyes. She imagined Nicholas riding over the ridge, silhouetted by the moon's light, his velvet coat billowing behind him, his tall collar pulled tight against the cold. Her mind filled with dread. She stretched and strained against the bindings till her wrists were raw. A faint smell of iron hovered in the room as blood oozed from her wrists and trickled off the ends of her fingers. She heard the faint drip as a drop of the blood fell to the floor. With deep mournful tones, the clock struck midnight, as the tip of one finger struck the curled metal of the trigger.

She didn't realize until that moment that the trigger had been her goal all along.

The wind rapped against the window, but it was the sound of galloping hooves that urged Bess on. The soldiers perked up, hearing the unmistakable echo on the frozen road. The lane glittered like a gypsy's ribbon as Nicholas crowned the rise. Bess took a last deep breath and squeezed the trigger.

Curses flew around the room and Barker shouted orders. Bess gasped at the blinding pain in her chest. She lifted her eyes to the window and watched as Nicholas reined in his stallion and fled to the east. She smiled as her head drooped over the musket, blood pooling warmly at her feet.

Bess felt no warmth, no cold, no heaviness. It was as if the bindings that had held her tight to the bedpost were suddenly released. She turned at the sound of her father's wail. He knelt in the doorjamb, doubled over as if in great pain. Tears glistened on her father's stubbled cheeks. His clothes were disheveled as if he had been in a tavern brawl. Bess couldn't find a memory for the sudden change in his appearance. She rushed to him, to offer comfort, but her outstretched hand did not touch him as she had known touch before. Together they drew a sharp breath of surprise.

"Bess?" He reached out a shaking hand.

"I am here, Father," she answered. But she could tell by the sorrow lining his face that he could not hear her. Could he feel her, though? Feel her spirit that wavered before him? Her arms longed to twine around his broad shoulders.

"I'm so sorry, Bess. I should've let Nicholas take you away from here a long time ago. He wanted to, but I wasn't ready to let you go." Her father's voice was choked by sobs that wracked his body. He covered his face with his hands.

Barker grabbed her father's arm and jerked him to his feet. "Where is he? Where did ride off to?"

53

"How am I to know?" her father said. "A high-wayman tells no one where he is headed or the road he rides. You murdered my sweet Bess for nothing."

"Murder?" Barker released her father's arm. "I did not murder your daughter. She pulled the trigger herself, to warn the thief."

"You gave her the trigger to pull."

Bess glided to the window. She did not bother to walk around Barker, and she felt him shiver as she passed through him. The candle still burnt in the window and her heart was heavy for her father, but her Nicholas lived. She pinched the wick with two fingers and doused the small flame. A thin trail of smoke rose, curling against the windowpane. "I love you, Bess," her father whispered.

"I love you too, Da," Bess whispered back.

She found him the next day.

The redcoats had run him down like a fox slaughtered in the hunt. He and his horse were left in the road, a bloody warning to those who defied the crown. The spirit of his horse was already free from its earthly constraints. He snuffled Bess with his broad nose and pawed Nicholas. Bess shook Nicholas's shoulder. "Time to ride, my love."

His eyes blinked open and squinted at her brightness. Bess reached for his hands and pulled him from his corpse. "No, don't look back, look at me."

Bess whistled a tune. The same he would whistle at her window, and his expression began to clear. The horse put his nose under Nicholas's hand and demanded a pat.

"Are we dead?" Nicholas asked.

"Of course. But we are together," answered Bess.

And still of a winter's night, they say, when the wind
is in the trees,
When the moon is a ghostly galleon tossed upon cloudy seas,
When the road is a ribbon of moonlight over the purple moor,
A highwayman comes riding—
Riding—riding—
A highwayman comes riding, up to the old inn-door.
Over the cobbles he clatters and clangs in the dark inn-yard;
He taps with his whip on the shutters, but all is locked and barred;
He whistles a tune to the window, and who should be waiting there
But the landlord's black-eyed daughter, Bess,
the landlord's daughter
Plaiting a dark red love knot into her long black hair.
-The Highwayman by Alfred Noyes, 1906

Gilded Tongues

For Ursula LeGuin whose short story, The Ones Who Walk Away from Omelas, *inspired this one.*

I hoisted myself onto the horse's silky chestnut back, using a fistful of mane to pull up my slight weight. My long golden hair twisted and tangled in the breeze that snapped the banners marking the racecourse. The mare's shoulder muscles bunched underneath my nakedness, the only orna-mentation of my body the garland of flowers draped over my breast. Only the power of the sun's rays and the steamy warmth of my eager mount kept me from shivering when the wind stretched out its delicate fingers to caress my skin. I was the symbol of summer. I was Juno. I was Aestas. I was Creiddylad.

My mother stood in the crowd, waving to me, proud of her daughter sitting atop the largest mare in the city. I tried to look happy, joyous even, but the feeling wouldn't come. It had left me days ago. At best I could feel contentment; at ease with the decision I had made, and yet uncomfortable in my new role. Shadows of the future frolicked at the edges of my vision, making melancholy leaps into the unknown.

The mare tossed her head and pranced with anticipation. I clenched my thighs tighter around her ribs. The excitement of the other horses, and maids astride them, was palpable. A cacophony of sound burst forth, like a cote of doves finally released from captivity, and the mare quickly moved to the front of the herd. I leaned forward into the fragrant wind and let the mare take her head, leaving behind the roaring crowds that had gathered for the Festival of the Sun.

The course took us out of the sparkling city and past the marina with its weathered, whitewashed decks, through the salt-laden air. I let the mare run until she had put us a league ahead of the other contestants, away from witnessing eyes. Then I reined her in, steering the horse into the shade of the forest that had lured only a few others before me.

I turned at the sound of thunder rolling down the mountainside, but it was only the others, flying past without a thought or worry of what had happened to their goddess.

Dismounting, I led the mare down the path I'd marked the day before. Narrow red ribbons tied to the thin branches of trees and frail stems of forest flowers showed me the way to the stone arch that marked the beginning of the old trail. The arch was no more than a ruin, a shadow of a fairy tale. The trail was overgrown and narrow. No one had come this way for many years, yet it was my decision. My choice. I thought of my mother, proudly waving, and a pain pulled at my chest. It was the same pain I felt when, as the one chosen to be the goddess, I'd looked upon the boy. The boy who lived in the cupboard, my city's own Pandora's box. The boy, who, in his fragile body, held all the sorrows of our world. The boy who was forced to know the truth unveiled.

I looked at him and I knew that the truth I had clung to, like a child at his mother's breast, was merely an invention brought forth from gilded tongues. The boy in the cupboard was my brother. My brother who, I was told years before, had passed to the gods shortly after his fourth birthday.

Passed to the gods

Eternally happy in a city more perfect than our own

And shouldn't we be glad for him?

They said.

Chosen by the gods

They said.

Lies embroidered into the fabric of our lives by the tongues of serpents. Threads spun of mirrored glass. I know this now. I think I knew it then, but the bright smiles of my mother and the elders of the city, hidden beneath their ancient, brocaded velvet robes, disguised the truth of his death as they disguise the truth of our being.

It wasn't even death, but something worse. How does one give up a child? How was he chosen? Why was he chosen? These questions took up an uneasy residence in my mind.

Would I ever know the answers?

Stolen Away

I plunged forward on the trail, into the unknown, heady, almost drunk, from the scent of the earth. Damp leaves, clinging moss and tender blooms perfumed the forest. Toward dusk the mare and I stopped at a brook, both dipping our heads into the water that meandered over pebbles shinning just beneath the surface. I was weary and chilled, the garland of flowers doing little to conserve the heat of my body. I climbed onto my mount to share the warmth that she freely gave and wrapped my hair about me like a cloak. I began to wonder if I had chosen rightly, to leave the warmth and comfort of home and city, but the mare plodded on, faithful to the path.

The Kelpie's Song

For Anne
Thank you for the inspiration.

The rough wool fibers slipped through my fingers. The whir of the spindle filled the chamber. It was a sound one grew used to and forgot was there, like the waves lapping the shore when one lived seaside. It was a small sound, but it filled the silence.

Pulling the shawl tighter around my shoulders, I twisted the last of the fibers I'd gathered from the fall shearing. The bats slumbering deep in the chamber stirred. High-pitched clicks echoed off the cave walls. Gathering the dark colored thread from the floor, I stuffed it into the small grass basket and stood, stretching stiff muscles. The sun hovered just above the horizon, it's gold-orange hue painting a footpath for the faeries to dance on the sea surface.

Pressing my hand against the ache in my back from the weight of my rounded belly, I strode toward the gaping mouth of the cave. The tangy scent of the sea brushed against my face as the wind rushed up the cliff like a dragon soaring on icy wings. The waves below sang against the rocks, a slow Selkie lullaby, the words lost to countless generations. A herd of seals gathered on the rocks below, huddled in dark masses. They called out when they saw me, barking in short yips and lengthy groans.

My toes curled around the sharp ledges of rock as I picked my way down to the shore. The narrow, spiraling path barely managed to cling to the vertical cliff. One misstep and my babe and I would be dancing with Barinthus, the sea god of old.

As my fingers ran over the soft patches of deep green moss rooted into the cliff face, I wondered if he'd come tonight.

Stolen Away

I strolled over the narrow beach and up a small grassy incline. The door of the small seaside cottage squeaked. Setting my spinning on the table I lit a candle and set it in the window that faced the bay. The tide rolled in as the sun sank.

I scraped the coals in the hearth and tossed some dry kelp weed onto them, watching them smolder and burst into a small yellow flame. Placing a peat brick into the fire I rubbed my arms, eager for the warmth to fill the room. Fetching the threads from the basket, I approached the mantle on the loom. I'd labored over it for nine months.

I'd spun every thread. Dyed every color. Woven every strand. There wasn't a single flaw.

Today would be my last for spinning. The thread in the basket was enough to finish the weaving. Weaving was a skill that took me months to learn, as I had no mentor other than my own memory. And the memories of my mother pushing the shuttle were as hard to capture as the light from a will-o-the-wisp.

The back of the mantle was a portrayal of my love for a kelpie; a dark horse with a flowing mane of waterweeds.

Legend passed down for centuries taught us the kelpie was dangerous, luring innocents to a watery death. But my kelpie was different.

I was four summers old the first time we met. My mother had been gathering crabs and sea bird eggs and I had wandered away. Lost, and crying, I saw him near a cave entrance.

Big.

Bold.

Beautiful.

I was just about to stroke his velvet nose, when I was snatched from behind and hauled up from the sandy earth.

Never touch a kelpie.

She whispered fiercely in my ear, her grip on my waist tighter than a crab's pinch.

But I couldn't forget those deep brown eyes.

I was 7 the next time we met. It was autumn and the cliffs above were frosted over. I was headed toward our cottage with a basketful of seaweed washed up by the previous nights storm when a heavy fog tumbled over the waves. A dark shape emerged, nickering and blowing.

Stolen Away

My kelpie.

I froze in place, trembling inside. My mother's warning echoed in my thoughts.

Never touch a kelpie.

My eyes clenched shut.

His muzzle grazed my cheek.

My fingers tightened around the handle of the basket. The rhythmic drip of water from his mane buried itself in my mind.

Bum-ba-da, dum-ba-da, bum-ba-da, dum-ba-da, bum-ba-da, dum-ba-da, dum, dum, dum, dum.

I stood, entranced as he sang to me, my grip loosening, my eyes opening to gaze at his sleek dark hair. His warm breath tickled the back of my neck and sent shivers through my body.

And then he galloped away.

It was nine years before I saw him again but I had dreamed of him every night, his song forever playing in the back of my mind.

On the eve of my sixteenth birthday my mother passed into the otherworld, leaving me alone in this one. I wrapped her in linens and carried her frail body to the shore. The tide was out as I laid her on the seabed, piling large rocks around her. Then I sat on the beach, knees pulled tight to my chest, and watched the sea welcome her as the tide returned, my warm tears mixing with the water as it reached for shore.

As the moon rose above the waves he returned.

Never touch a kelpie.

But there was nothing left for me in this world.

His song floated in my mind. As he approached I stood, deep brown eyes seizing my gaze and holding me captive.

He circled, snorting and blowing, as if he was trying to intimidate me with his size and strength. But I was not so easily frightened. I stretched my fingers out to caress his neck. His muscles bunched and twitched under my touch. I sang his song in clear, high notes and he nuzzled my neck with his velvet soft muzzle. His warm breath smelled of the briny sea. I closed my eyes and leaned into his chest, his watery mane falling over my shoulder.

Oh, to feel love for a man as I did for my kelpie.

He snorted and pranced away. Shaking his head and pawing at the salt-laden bridle on his head. I reached for it, my fingers grasping the straps, pulling with all my strength. My kelpie struggled free and collapsed into the breaking water.

The waves washed over him. My heartbeat quickened, my blood pounded behind my ears. Relief rolled over me when he stirred, a black mass in the moonlight. But what stood up from the beach was no horse.

The bridle fell from my grasp and I averted my eyes from his naked form. The heat of a blush crawled up my neck and settled in my cheeks.

His thumb caressed my lips as he gathered my face in his hands and forced me to look at him. His deep brown eyes searched mine.

We have only this one night.

My hands gripped his forearms as my cheek leaned into his palm.

Enchantments must be mended in specific ways.

His husky voice vibrated my soul and sent waves through my body.

I searched his face for more information, but he could give none. We didn't speak as he led me to the cottage I'd shared with my mother and showed me the love of a man.

In the morning he was gone. I spent the next three weeks roaming the beach and calling him by name.

Roanen

When he didn't come back I got angry and hurled curses at him into the waves of the sea he had emerged from.

And then I cried.

Two months after he'd left I found a book wrapped in leather and tied with a faded ribbon, shoved under my mother's bed. I sliced the ribbon with a knife and unwrapped the package. My mother's handwriting filled the pages. A record of her life scrawled across the parchment. Memories of me as a babe, her full heart as I grew up strong, and then the apprehension. Worries about the kelpie; pages full of records and sightings. The moon stage, the month, the season, even how warm it had been or if there had been a fog over the sea. My mother had seen him more than I. Did she keep me from him deliberately? I started to get angry all over again.

And then I flipped to the last page.

It was a message from my mother, clearly intended for me to find after her death.

Never touch a kelpie. For he will take your heart when he returns to the sea. Thankfully, your father gave half of my heart back when he gave me you. You are a kelpie's child.

My hand rested on the babe that was within me. A kelpie's child.

The rest of the message told me what I must do to break the enchantment, to release the man from the water horse if that was my true desire. I hoped my ending would be different than hers.

I pushed the shuttle tight against the last row of weaving and sighed. The cloak was finished. Carefully I removed it from the loom and folded it in half. My hands shook as I threaded a needle and seamed the sleeves from the wrist, curving through the underarm, and down the side. I knotted and clipped the thread.

The cloak was as beautiful and as dark as his kelpie coat. Knotted lines formed a border around the edge. An image of a kelpie was worked on the back, his long tail, twisting through his legs.

The moon was a shining orb heavy with possibility. The stars winked and twinkled between the scattered clouds. The waves rolled in softly onto the shore. I draped the cloak over my arm and walked out of the little cottage.

My hair tangled in the wind like a wild horse's mane. My toes tingled as the cold sea washed over them. I sang his song, the notes echoing off the cliff face and carrying over the water.

I sang and sang, until my voice was hoarse and my tongue tasted like brine, but he did not come. Sinking into the sand the cold fingers of the sea grabbed at my knees. Clouds obscured the stars and blocked the silvery light of the moon. Warm tears slid down my face and fell into the water and still I sang, my voice cracking and rough. The wind rushed around me, carrying my song further.

He did not come.

I buried my head in the cloak and sobbed until I could cry no more. My limbs were weak and my body trembled.

The clouds drifted away and once again the moon lit the shore and made the white crested waves shimmer. A soft whicker drifted in the air. A warm rush of air grazed my neck. Goosebumps erupted on my arms as I rose and turned, throwing my arms around the neck of my kelpie.

Roanen

I stroked his mane and kissed his velvet nose. My fingers gripped the bridle and I struggled to remove it. He shook his head and wrenched it loose. Dropping the bridle, I threw the mantle over his back as he collapsed onto the sand.

I held my breath as I waited, counting my heartbeats. Slowly the form of the horse shifted under the cloak. The legs drew in as the hooves split into toes and fingers. Water flowed from his mane, leaving his glossy dark hair dry. He pushed his arms through the sleeves and grabbed the bridle as he stood. He flung it into the sea, watching as it sank below the waves. Then he turned to me and opened his arms.

I threw myself into his embrace our lips meeting with fierce desire. He tasted of kelp and brine and promises. His hand followed the contours of my round belly. The babe was restless under his touch.

"Will you come with me?" he asked.

"Anywhere," I vowed.

About the Author

Jennifer Carson is a mom, wife, author and designer. She lives in New Hampshire with her family and many four legged friends. She grew up on a steady diet of Muppet movies and Renaissance faires and was occaisionaly caught reading under the blankets with a flashlight.

In April 2009, Jennifer received the NE-SCBWI Ruth Landers Glass Scholarship. Jennifer's first book, *To Find A Wonder,* was published in 2009 by L&L Dreamspell and was adapted into a musical and performed at the New London Barn Playhouse in August 2010. Her latest novel, *Hapenny Magick* is a delightful read-aloud for all ages.

Jennifer also publishes sewing patterns and is an award-winning fiber artist. You can find out more about her writing at her website:

www.thedragoncharmer.com.